D0580623

Spunky Spot

HAPPY READING!

This book is especially for:

_____

Suzanne Tate,
Author—
brings fun and
facts to us in her
Nature Series.

James Melvin,
Illustrator—
brings joyous life
to Suzanne Tate's
characters.

Suzanne and James in costume

Spunky Spot
A Tale of One Smart Fish

Suzanne Tate

Illustrated by James Melvin

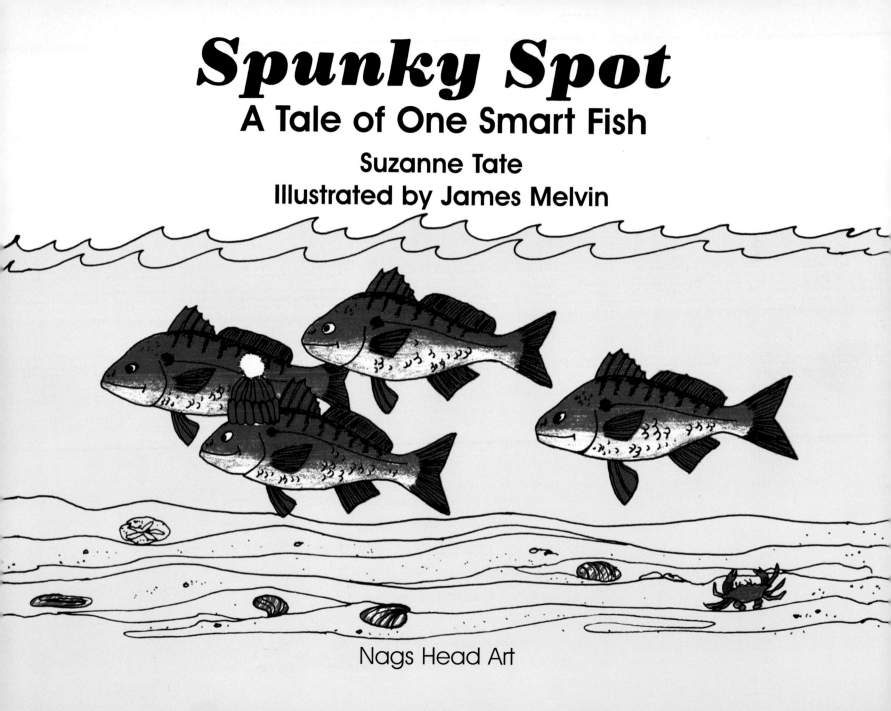

Nags Head Art

To Daddy
who urged me to write

Library of Congress Control Number 88-63784
ISBN 978-0-9616344-6-9
ISBN 0-9616344-6-4
Published by
Nags Head Art, Inc., P.O. Box 2149, Manteo, NC 27954
Copyright © 1989 by Nags Head Art, Inc.
Revised 2005

All Rights Reserved
Printed in the United States of America

Spunky Spot was a little fish.
He was a kind of fish called Spot.
Spunky had gold and silver sides.
And he had a black spot on each side.

Spots swim in schools.
They feed on the bottom of the water.
There they find good things to eat —
tiny clams and shrimp and crabs.

When Spunky Spot was very little,
he couldn't wait to be in the school.
He wanted to learn to read.

As the days went by, he swam and ate
on the bottom.

Soon he was big enough to swim
in the school of Spots.

Spunky met his teacher in the school —
Miss Spiffy Spot.
She was kind and fine. (She was spiffy!)

In the school, he learned to read:
See Spot.
See Spot swim.

It was exciting to learn to read!

But Spunky learned many other things
from Miss Spiffy Spot. She taught him
how to feed along the bottom of the water.

"Stick your nose right in the mud,"
Miss Spiffy Spot said.
"Maybe you can find a little soft crab
or clam buried there."

Spunky did as his teacher told him to do.
He was a good little Spot in the school.

Soon he scooped up and ate a little clam.
"Oh, what a tasty morsel," Spunky said.

Miss Spiffy Spot knew there were
other things for Spunky to learn.

Very important things —
like saying *no* to WORMS.

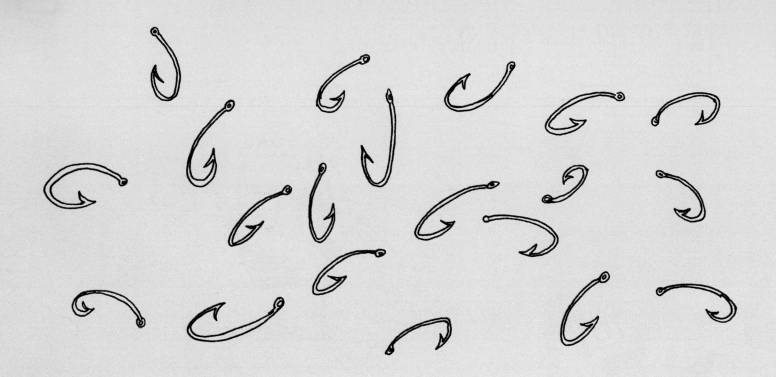

Now WORMS were tasty to Spots.
But inside WORMS,
there were hooks.
(Hooks just right to catch Spots.)

"Just say *no* to WORMS,"
Miss Spiffy Spot said to Spunky.

NO!

Spunky wanted to listen to his teacher.
He knew that she knew best.

But Spunky was young.
And he wanted to be daring.
He wanted to try new things.

One day Spunky was swimming
in the school.
They were near the Little Bridge.

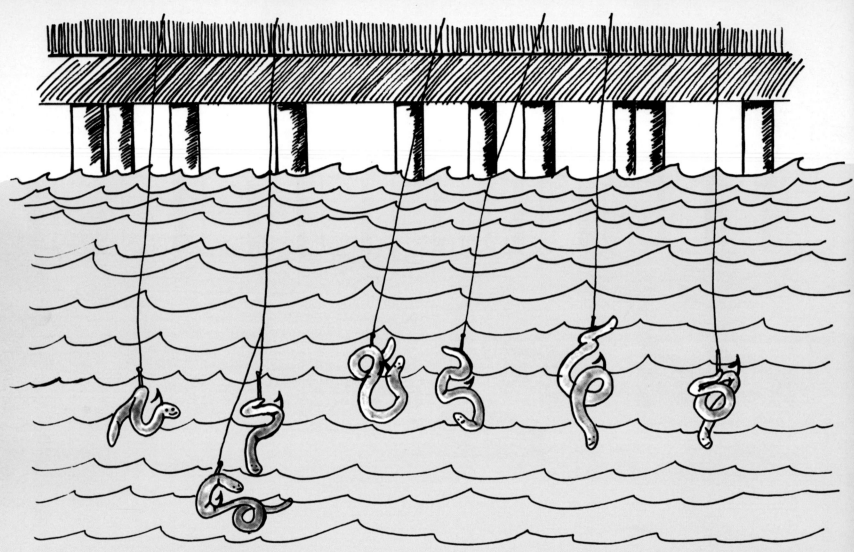

The Little Bridge was a tempting place for Spots.
They could find lots of WORMS there
in the water.

But the WORMS had a catch to them!
Hidden inside were those shiny, sharp hooks.

Some of the Spots were reckless.
They didn't say *no* to WORMS.
They would swim up close to them
and nibble a tasty bite.

Spunky watched them one day.
He wanted to try WORMS.
He wondered if he could just
take a nibble.

"Surely that won't hurt me," he thought to himself.

But then he remembered Miss Spiffy Spot's warning: "Just say *no* to WORMS."

About that time, he saw one of the Spots
nibble a WORM.

Suddenly, that Spot was swooshed away!
He was gone — just like that.

There was a catch to the WORM!
And that Spot was in a bad spot.

Spunky knew for sure now:
better safe than sorry.
"I'll stick to old favorites,"
he sang as he swam away.

"Little clams and shrimp look better to me
than ever before. I'll always say *no* to WORMS!"

Miss Spiffy Spot came swimming up to Spunky!
"Now you see what happens
when you're hooked," she said.

"I'm glad to see you have the spunk to say *no!*"

Flossie smiled.
She was happy.
Floyd was now flat as a flounder.

Floyd swam back to Green Island.
He soon found his Mama Flossie.

"Look at me," he said proudly.
"I am fat. I am flat. Both of my eyes are topside.
Now my friends in the school
won't make fun of me!"

Mark enjoyed watching the changes in Floyd.
But one day, he decided to turn him loose.

"Goodbye, little fish," Mark said.
"Goodbye, and thank you," said Floyd.
But Mark didn't hear him.

Mark kept Floyd well-fed.
Floyd began to grow fatter and wider.

He leaned on one side until he was flat.
One of his eyes moved!
Then both of his eyes were topside!

But it wasn't so bad.
There were lots of tiny shrimp there
to feed on.

He couldn't swim away.
Floyd was trapped in Mark's aquarium.

But something was fishy!
Something was wrong.
When Floyd tried to swim fast,
he bumped into something hard.

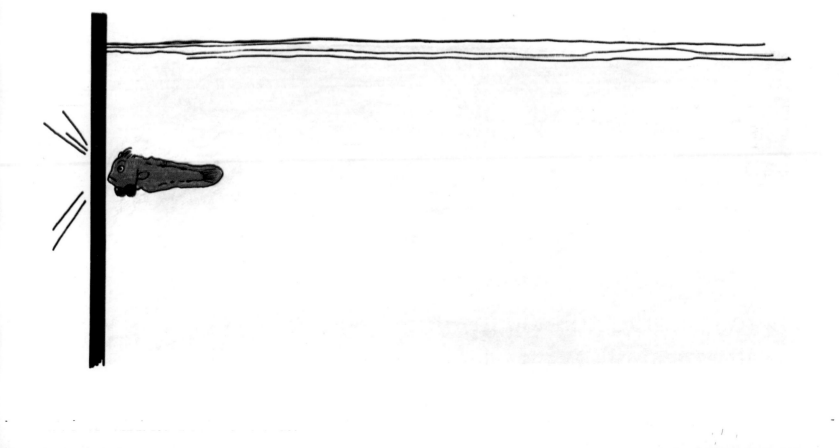

There was grass to hide in
just like around Green Island.
"This is a nice place," thought Floyd at first.

Mark scooped up Floyd
and put him in a glass box.
There was plenty of water and sand.

"What have I here?" said Mark.
"A baby fish — just right for my aquarium."

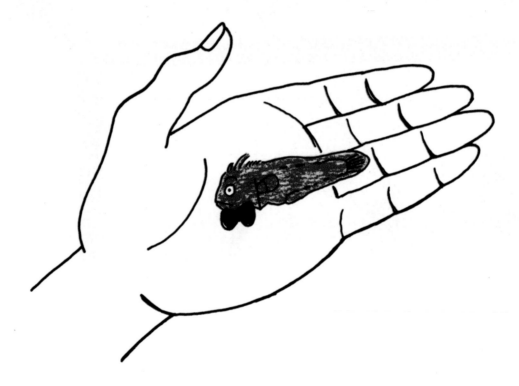

It wasn't a big NET.
But Floyd was caught in it.

Floyd was so busy
that he didn't see the NET.

A boy named Mark was sweeping it
along the bottom.

So Floyd swam away again
in the school of baby flounders.
He caught tiny shrimp
and tried to be happy.

Flossie swam up to him. "Don't worry," she said.
"You will soon be fat and flat!
Both your eyes will be topside.
And you will begin to swim on one side!"

"How can that ever be true?" cried Floyd.
"You will see," Flossie said.

"Why can't I be like the others?"
Floyd cried softly.
He didn't want the other flounders to know.

"One-eye, one-eye," they called to Floyd.
"You're not fat, you're not flat!" It made Floyd feel bad.
He wanted to look like the other flounders.

The other little flounders were babies, too.
But they were older than Floyd.

They had already become tiny flat fish.
They swam on one side.
And both their eyes were topside.

One day Floyd was floundering around.
He was in a school of little flounders.
They were catching tiny shrimp
near a place called Green Island.

Floyd Flounder was Flossie's baby.
But he didn't look like her.
He swam upright. He was round and not flat.
And he had an eye on each side of his head.

When shrimp or little fish came along,
she sprang to life.
And she grabbed a quick lunch!

Flossie could change herself —
so that she looked like the bottom
she was lying on.

Both of Flossie's eyes were on her topside.
She could lie on the bottom —
and see everything good to eat swimming by.

Flossie belonged to the flatfish family.
Like all of them, she lived at the bottom of the sea.

She liked to live there.

Flossie Flounder was a flat fish.
She was fat as well as flat.

To Scott
who inspires more stories

Library of Congress Control Number 88-92679
ISBN 978-0-9616344-5-2
ISBN 0-9616344-5-6
Published by
Nags Head Art, Inc., P.O. Box 2149, Manteo, NC 27954
Copyright ©1989 by Nags Head Art, Inc.
Revised 2005

All Rights Reserved
Printed in the United States of America

Flossie Flounder
A Tale of Flat Fish

Suzanne Tate
Illustrated by James Melvin

Nags Head Art

HAPPY READING!

This book is especially for:

_____

Suzanne Tate,
Author—
brings fun and
facts to us in her
Nature Series.

James Melvin,
Illustrator—
brings joyous life
to Suzanne Tate's
characters.

Suzanne and James in costume

D0580624

Flossie Flounder